**W9-CKS-678**

OTHER YEARLING BOOKS YOU WILL ENJOY:

*Nate the Great,* MARJORIE WEINMAN SHARMAT
*Nate the Great Goes Undercover,* MARJORIE WEINMAN SHARMAT
*Somebody Stole Second,* LOUISE MUNRO FOLEY
*The Thing at the Foot of the Bed,* MARIA LEACH
*The Case of the Elevator Duck,* POLLY BERRIEN BERENDS
*Flat Stanley,* JEFF BROWN
*The Witch's Egg,* MADELEINE EDMONDSON
*Chocolate Fever,* ROBERT KIMMEL SMITH
*The Secret of the Sachem's Tree,* F. N. MONJO
*The Beetle Bush,* BEVERLY KELLER

# The Case of the Missing Ten Speed Bike

by John Shearer

Pictures by Ted Shearer

A Yearling Book

# Billy Jo Jive Super Private Eye

**To Schatzi, the Sunset of my life.**

Published by
Dell Publishing Co., Inc.
1 Dag Hammarskjold Plaza
New York, New York 10017

Yearling ® TM 913705, Dell Publishing Co., Inc.

ISBN: 0-440-41017-7

Reprinted by arrangement with Delacorte Press
Printed in the United States of America
Second Dell Printing—November 1978

FL

**M**y name is Billy Jo Jive. In my turf, people go by the last part, so call me Jive.

I'm the best, the bravest, the smartest Private Eye in the world. I'm so bad, I hipped Dick Tracy and John Shaft's daddy to what was happenin'.

There is nothin' I can't find. I've found a bat for my brother, a wool scarf for my sister and sunglasses for my ma.

Anyway, in my latest gig, I deal with this real fine sister. Susie Sunset is her name. The first time Sunset and I met, I was cruisin' cool on my old red Crime

Fighter bike. I spotted this chick cryin'
like rain. I rode up and said, "Say baby,
what's wrong with your head?"

"Don't call me baby. My name is Sunset!" she said. "What's yours?"

"I'm Billy Jo Jive, Super Private Eye. I'm faster than light, stronger than steel and cooler than ice. Wipe the clouds from your eyes and tell me what's wrong!"

"Oh, Jive, I borrowed my big brother Sammy's Super Cool Blue Ten Speed Bike. I lost it this morning. Sammy is at camp but he'll be back on Friday. If I don't find that bike, he'll be mad as thunder!"

"Say, isn't Saturday the day of the big bike race? The one they have in the park every year?"

"Yes, Jive, and Sammy won that race last year, and the year before that. But he won't win this Saturday without his bike!"

"Have no fear," I said, "Jive is here. I'll help you find those super cool wheels."

Sunset was glad to have me on the case. We went to track down some clues.

As we got up to Sunset's pad I knew this was the biggest crime scene I had ever seen.

"Your pad must be the scene of the crime," I said.

"Wow," Sunset said. "You are a great Private Eye. How did you know this was my house?"

"Well, I just spotted the cut bike chain on the fence. It wasn't hard to figure out."

But I needed more clues. I looked
up the street and down the block. I
checked round the corner. There was a
group of stick ball playin', bike ridin'
dudes down the way.

"Keep out of sight," I said to Sunset.
"I'm goin' to check out those big guys."
I was over to the dudes in a flash. "A
friend of mine lost some fancy wheels

the other day," I said. "Any of you dudes know anything about it?"

None of them had anything to tell me. As I turned away, the baddest of them, Dynamite Jones, called out, "Sorry I can't help you, little brother, but if I hear anything at all I'll let you know."

Then another big guy, Sideburns Harris, said, "Right on, brother, now go back and play with your toys."

When I found Sunset later she was rappin' heavy to a neighbor lady. "What did the boy look like?" Sunset asked.

"Why, I'm really not sure," the lady said. "I could only see his back. And my eyes get a little tired late in the day."

Tired eyes, late in the day, this was no lead.

We thanked the lady and were about to split up for the day when Sunset said, "Well, we can be sure of one thing! It was a boy who took my brother's bike."

That night I made plans. All we had to do was find one dude out of the nine hundred in the neighborhood.

Next morning I left for Sunset's house right after breakfast. On the way I ran into Dynamite Jones. He was cruisin' along on a red racer. When he saw me, he slowed down. "Say, Jive, I think I saw the ten speed bike you're lookin' for. Meet me in a half hour at the abandoned building around the corner."

I split to Sunset's. When I got there, she was good and mad! "Sure did take you long enough to get here. I've been waitin' for you for an hour!"

"Listen Sunset," I said, "I got a good lead, so jump on behind and let's go."

It seemed like no sooner had I pushed my throttle to full speed when I spotted the old building and Dynamite Jones parked out front. We pulled up beside him.

"Well, is that the ten speed?" he asked.

There was a broken blue bike in the alley.

Sunset ran up to it. She looked at it from the front and from the rear. She tried beepin' the horn and spun around a rusty wheel. She came back to us lookin' real sad.

"No," she said. "That's not my brother's bike. But thanks anyway for tryin' to help."

"Got to get back on the case," I said. "Let's go, Sunset."

We followed everything that left the
block. We went to where the garbage
men take the garbage, where the mail-
men take the mail and where the tow

trucks take the cars. No Blue Bike. We
shadowed the milkman, the gasman and
the newsboy. Still no Blue Bike.

At the end of the day, Sunset and I were feelin' mighty low. The race was only two days away. Sammy Sunset would be home from camp tomorrow and there would be no Blue Ten Speed Bike. He had won that race for two years straight. If we didn't find those wheels, he'd be out of the race this year.

The next day I went over to Sunset's. She was really worried. "Jive, what are we goin' to do? Sammy is goin' to be back late today, and we have no bike. He loves that bike. Check out this book he keeps of the races he's been in!"

Sunset handed me her brother's scrapbook. In it were a lot of clips of all the past races.

We looked through the book
together. All of a sudden it hit me.
"Sunset, do you see what I see?"

"Sure do, Jive. Dynamite Jones came in second to my brother in the last two races. I thought there was somethin' strange about him all along. You remember he knew the bike was a ten speed without bein' told."

"That's right," I said. "I bet his helpin' us was just somethin' to throw us off."

Then Sunset had an idea. "Jive, stop runnin' your mouth for a minute and listen to this. You remember the abandoned building that Dynamite took us to?"

"Right on," I said. "That would be a good place to leave a bike."

"Let's go check it out," Sunset said. She was real excited.

The empty building looked real spooky. The door was boarded up, but

Sunset and I spotted a half-open window
on the second floor. It was an easy climb.
We went right up the fire escape.

Inside, I pulled out my Crime
Fighter flashlight.

The steps creaked and groaned as
we went down the stairs. It sure was a
scary scene.

The basement was dark and creepy. It had a lot of hangin' lights and drippin' pipes. Then somethin' strange caught Sunset's eye.

"Say, Jive, shine your flashlight over there." She pushed my hand to the right. There was a door with a lock and chain. "There must be somethin' very important behind that door," I said.

Suddenly we heard someone com-
in' down the stairs. We hid behind some
garbage cans. I turned off my Crime
Fighter. We waited.

A figure came toward us. We couldn't see his face even though he had a match in his hand. But it sure looked like Dynamite Jones. Slowly, he moved to the locked door. He unlocked the heavy padlock and the creakin', squeakin' door swung open. In the faint

flicker of the match light what did we
see! The Blue Ten Speed Bike! Sammy
Sunset's stolen wheels! Then, the
match went out.

This was our chance. There was some rope next to the garbage can. I grabbed it. Sunset and I jumped on the figure. We had him tied up in a flash. I turned on my Crime Fighter to see if I was right about who had stolen Sammy's Super Cool Blue Ten Speed Bike.

Sure enough, it was Dynamite.

"I guess bein' number two, two years in a row was just a little too much for him," Sunset said.

While I held on to Dynamite, Sunset ran out to get help. She came

back with the guys and I put my Crime
Fighter Light on Dynamite.

"We don't want to see you around
here no more," I said. "And if Sammy
ever finds out you stole his wheels,
you're gonna be in bigger trouble."

We left Dynamite with the guys and got the ten speed bike back to Sunset's pad just in time. Sammy Sunset was comin' up the block.

"What you kids been up to?" he asked.

Sunset looked at me. I looked at Sunset. What Sammy didn't know wouldn't hurt him. Anyhow, now he could win that big race tomorrow. Thanks to me and Sunset.

"You're a great Private Eye, Jive," Sunset whispered.

As I waved good-bye to Sunset I knew I had to be the best, the bravest, the smartest Private Eye in the world. And Susie Sunset sure made a good partner.

Now I just had to get home. My mother would be mad if she knew I was out so long!